MELTDOWN TOWN

by Sean Tulien

www.12StoryLibrary.com

12-Story Library is an imprint of Peterson Publishing Company and Press Room Editions.

Produced for 12-Story Library by Red Line Editorial

Photographs ©: Shutterstock Images, cover, 3

Cover Design: Laura Polzin

ISBN
978-1-63235-165-4 (hardcover)
978-1-63235-204-0 (paperback)
978-1-62143-256-2 (hosted ebook)

Library of Congress Control Number: 2015934309

Printed in the United States of America
Mankato, MN
June, 2015

PROLOGUE

The man in the white lab coat didn't stop walking when holographic red Xs appeared in front of him.

He didn't stop walking when the alarms began to blare.

He didn't stop when he reached the irradiated zone.

He didn't stop when he became dizzy, when his skin began to blister, or when he began to vomit blood.

The farther he walked, the stronger the radiation got, and the faster he'd die. The sooner he'd escape Asheville. Radiation was closing in on the town, and like a handful of other people, he chose a quick death over a slow one.

He kept going when blindness set in, when his limbs went numb, and when his flesh began to slough off his bones.

Eventually, when he crumpled to the ground, the alarms went silent.

CHAPTER
1

Liam rubbed his hands together for warmth. The night air was chilly, and he'd been standing at the edge of Old Asheville waiting for Grace for nearly an hour.

This was nothing new. Grace was never on time. But Liam didn't mind. Of the two of them, she was the outgoing one, and he enjoyed tagging along on her adventures. She had a knack for drawing Liam out of his shell and making him take risks, whether he wanted to or not. And besides, exploring the remains of a forgotten section of town was worth the wait.

Just then, two small hands covered Liam's eyes from behind.

"Guess who?" chirped a familiar voice.

Liam spun around and said, "Took you long enough."

Grace let her head fall to one side. "Yeah, Dad was taking forever finishing his dinner, so I couldn't sneak out right away."

"Got your LED light?" Liam asked.

Graced clicked a button on the object hanging around her neck. A bright light burst out, illuminating the area. "Yep!"

Liam laughed. "So what's the plan for tonight's adventure?"

Grace cocked an eyebrow. "You pick this time."

Without hesitating, Liam said, "The old Victorian."

Grace rolled her eyes. "What's it with you and that old mansion? But okay. Let's do it." She shoved Liam playfully. "Ladies first."

Liam turned to hide his face. He could never tell if Grace was flirting with him or mocking him. Either way, he blushed every time.

Heading south at a brisk pace, Liam asked, "So what'd you cook for your dad?"

"Veggie pot pie," Grace said. She leaned in to whisper, "The secret ingredient—lots of butter."

Liam smiled. The warmth of her breath against his neck made his heart beat faster.

They soon passed a dust-covered, rusted-out sports car.

"Pretty good shape for being seventy-some years old," he said. He glanced at Grace. "Why do you think no one comes here?"

"Besides the fact that we're not supposed to, you mean?" Grace said with a shrug. "I think it reminds people of the past. People would rather forget what happened."

Liam burst into forced laughter. "Forget? How could any of us forget? Between the irradiated zones we have to avoid and the worldwide energy crisis, how could anyone forget about the Kerrigan Reactor Meltdown?"

Grace stuck her tongue out at Liam. "That was way back in 2020. Life goes on. You spend too much time staring into the abyss of the past, and it'll swallow you up." She sighed. "Besides, why do you think *we* take these little trips?"

Liam hesitated. If he were honest, he'd say it was to spend time with Grace, but that'd just earn him an elbow in the ribs, some teasing, or worse.

"Better than homework," he half-lied.

Grace nodded at the remnants of a gas station. "I think it's a distraction. An escape." She shot Liam a furtive glance. "I mean, it's fun, too. But I get so sick of those gaudy radiation barriers and all the clean, white walls everywhere I look. It's like we're being forced to live in between death and boredom."

Liam got lost in thought. That tended to happen around Grace. She was a mix of a post-punk-rock philosopher and a know-it-all, but in a good way. Mostly. In any case, Grace was right. These trips were a distraction—from life, death, and everything in between.

As they walked on in silence, Liam observed the remains of what had once been known simply as Asheville, but was now called Old Asheville. Most of it was bordered by red holographic ribbons and alarm systems indicating irradiated zones, or RadZones. People had fled the area as soon as they could, even though this part of Asheville hadn't been in immediate danger from the Kerrigan Disaster of 2020. But no one wanted to risk staying.

The joke had been on them, though, since there really was nowhere to escape to. Soon after the Kerrigan Reactor in Asheville had its meltdown, other nuclear power plants around the world followed suit. Dr. Kerrigan, the man who'd designed the Asheville reactor—and the components that allowed power sharing across entire countries—hadn't protected the network well enough. Terrorist hackers had caused the Kerrigan meltdown. Their aim was to attack the United States, but since the nuclear plants around the world were all connected, a chain reaction occurred that plunged the planet into a worldwide energy crisis.

Millions died. Maybe billions. It was hard to know when your town was cut off from the rest of the world.

If New Asheville was a dying city, Old Asheville was already dead. Long dead. Deader than dead. The homes had been abandoned for more than seventy years. The area was off-limits to everyone, mostly because of the danger of radiation. But no one went there anyway. Except for Grace and Liam.

"Besides," Grace said, snapping Liam back to reality. "What's a better distraction from a doomed city than visiting an old one?"

Liam nodded. "Fair enough."

Grace kicked a chunk of brick down the weed-infested street.

"How much farther?" she asked.

"Two blocks down, one to the left," Liam said, realizing he'd just given Grace more proof he was obsessed with the old mansion.

Grace laughed; Liam cringed.

"I don't know why you're so infatuated with that overgrown dollhouse," she said.

Liam didn't respond.

"Okay, we're here," Grace said a moment later. "You're kind of spacey tonight. You okay?"

Liam smiled and looked up at the Victorian house with its tall, peaked roof.

"Am now," he said, stepping onto the porch. "Seems solid," he added, gently bouncing up and down.

"Good," Grace said.

She walked past him, opened the front door, and walked inside. Liam followed, scanning the area with his flashlight. The inside of the house was like a dusty museum; nothing had changed in the seven decades it'd been empty. Everything was in its right place. Sun streaming in through the windows had bleached the exposed areas of the hardwood floor. The musty, stale air made Liam's nose twitch.

Liam left the entryway and joined Grace in the living room. Hardbound, physical books lined the shelves along the walls. Liam had never actually read an analog novel since all of them were now digital.

"Did they really use all this space just for their books back then?" he wondered aloud.

"Yep," Grace said, picking one up. "I kinda like them. There's something about holding it in your hands. Like the words inside exist in the

SEAN TULIEN

real world instead of just the empty space inside a computer."

"I never thought of it that way," Liam said. He lifted a book from the shelves. "Sure is less efficient."

Grace plopped down in a leather chair, sending dust billowing out in all directions like a mushroom cloud. She trained her flashlight on the pages of the book and read.

Liam deposited his book back on the shelf and headed to the central staircase. The ornate handrails led him up into darkness.

Liam poked his flashlight inside the first room. A wooden cradle sat in one corner. Above it, a cluster of family photos decorated one wall, barely visible through the film of dust. A chill ran up his spine; he felt like a ghost wandering the halls of a long-dead family's memories. He turned and headed back to the stairs, following the footprints he'd made in the dust.

Halfway down the staircase, Grace's flashlight illuminated Liam's face. He held up his hand to block the glare.

"How was your book?" he asked.

"Great so far. Gonna take it with me."

Liam was about to object, but then he realized there was no point. It wasn't stealing if no one was alive to care.

"So what's it about?" Liam asked.

Grace shrugged and leaned on the handrail. It creaked.

Liam rolled his eyes. "Okay, then, who's the author?"

"Some lady named Ursula Le Guin," Grace said. "It's fantasy. Or maybe sci-fi."

"In other words, ultra-nerdy?" Liam teased.

Grace grinned and smacked Liam on the shoulder. He was about to pinch her forearm when a loud creak came from below. They looked down just in time to see the stairs crumble beneath their feet. They were plunged into darkness.

CHAPTER
2

Grace watched a sphere of light rapidly flickering on the walls of the basement. It took her a moment to realize it was her LED light spinning in circles on the floor. Grace tried to sit up, but she couldn't move her legs.

"Liam," she croaked.

Silence.

Broken chunks of wood were strewn everywhere.

"Liam!" Grace cried shakily.

A soft groan came from near her feet. She reached out and grabbed the LED. Liam was draped across her shins. His eyes narrowed in the glare of her flashlight.

"Are you okay?" Liam asked.

"Yeah," Grace said.

"What happened?" Liam asked, rubbing the back of his head.

"The stairs caved in," Grace said as if she were sharing news about the weather. "If you're okay, do you mind getting off of me?"

"Oh, right." Slowly, carefully, Liam lifted himself off Grace's legs and into a kneeling position.

Grace pulled her thighs in against her chest, wrapped her arms around her shins, and rested her chin on her knees. She felt each shin gingerly, discovering what were likely nasty bruises.

"Let's not do that again," she said.

Liam got back to his feet. "Agreed." He picked up his LED and smacked it a few times until it came back to life. "Thanks for cushioning my fall, by the way."

Grace chuckled. "What are friends for?"

Liam glanced up at the huge hole in the ceiling where the stairs had been. He sighed. The long-rotten wood had given way.

Liam tilted his head at her. "Seriously, though, are you okay?"

"Yeah," Grace said. She stood up slowly, wobbling a little. She'd definitely have some bruises. "Let's get outta here before something else collapses on us."

Liam hurried over to the only door in the cluttered room. He reached for the doorknob, turned it, and pulled. It didn't move. He pulled harder. Nothing. He put one leg on the wall, lowered his center of gravity, and yanked hard. It didn't budge.

"Um, I think it's locked," he said. "From the outside."

Grace groaned. "You've gotta be kidding me." She craned her neck, then shined her light at the edge of the ceiling. "Come give me a lift?"

Liam walked over, and crouching down, cupped his hands together. Grace slipped her foot into his grip, and he lifted her up. In one swift movement, she reached for the floorboards, grabbed hold, scurried up, and disappeared from view.

"Nice work," Liam said. "What about me?"

No response.

"Grace?"

Silence.

Pressure built in his chest. He swallowed his fear down and silently counted to ten.

"Grace," he said through clenched teeth. "Seriously, what's the plan here?"

Still nothing.

He jumped to reach the floorboards. The tips of his fingers only scraped against the edge.

"Grace!"

A slow creak came from behind him. He spun around to see Grace standing in the open doorway.

"Why are you freaking out?" she asked.

Liam shook his head. "For a second, I thought . . . never mind."

"Come on," Grace said, gesturing for Liam to follow. "Let's head home."

Together they walked up a stairway and out of the basement. Liam glanced over at the red holographic ribbon about 100 yards south of the house. It marked where above-normal levels of radiation began.

"I wonder if the family who lived here knows how lucky they were that the radiation didn't reach them."

"Who cares," Grace said, slowing her pace to walk next to Liam. "It's been seventy years. They're all dead now."

Liam tilted his head at Grace. Weird things came out of her mouth lately. Things that made him worry about her. She was tough to read for the most part, but the way her eye twitched sometimes was a dead giveaway that something was bugging her.

Grace pointed at the shimmering RadZone barrier. "I don't really feel like walking through the ruins again. Let's just follow the barrier toward the next RadZone pylon and head back to town from there."

Liam nodded. "Sounds good. Might take a little longer."

"Fine by me," Grace said, elbowing him in the arm.

"Ow," Liam said, smiling from ear to ear.

He couldn't think of anything clever to say back, so he just glanced out over the irradiated zone. The flickering red ribbon was much closer to the old Victorian than the last time they'd been nearby, but that was to be expected. All residents of New Asheville knew the barriers were being pushed by increasing radiation levels.

"The barrier's moving a bit," Liam said.

"Yeah," Grace said. "My dad figured out a few days ago that a crack in the Kerrigan Reactor is getting bigger."

Liam's eyes went wide. "Isn't that, like, bad?"

Grace smirked. "Yep."

"Then why didn't you tell me before now?" Liam asked.

Grace's face grew serious. "He told me not to tell anyone—even you."

"Is there any hope of plugging it up?"

Grace shrugged. "He didn't say." She pointed in the distance at a red, flashing dome atop a giant pillar. "Almost to the pylon."

Liam gawked at Grace. "Aren't you worried about getting irradiated? Dying? *Anything?*"

Grace sighed. "The encroachment is still pretty slow," she said tonelessly. "Unless it speeds up, it'll take a few more years for it to encompass Old Asheville."

"Yeah," Liam said. "Unless the crack in the reactor gets worse faster than your dad anticipates."

Grace nodded.

They were closer to the barrier now, maybe 100 feet away. Liam hadn't even realized they were nearing it—he'd just been following Grace.

"I just don't get how you're so calm about all this," he grumbled.

Grace started walking faster. Liam debated letting her walk away, but she was heading straight for the barrier. He quickened his pace to catch up.

"Did I say something wrong?" he called after her.

Grace said nothing. They were maybe fifty feet from the barrier now. Liam's eyes darted back and forth between the barrier and his best friend.

"Grace," he said, his voice cracking. "What did I say?"

Grace just walked faster. Liam half-ran to keep up, terror writ large on his face as they drew nearer and nearer to the RadZone. Red holographic Xs began to pop up.

When they were ten feet away from the barrier, Liam grabbed Grace by the shoulder.

"Grace, I'm sorry! Just tell me what's—"

"Shh!" she whispered.

She slowly extended her finger toward the RadZone. A phosphorescent green light was bobbing up and down inside the irradiated zone. Liam's jaw dropped. In silence, they watched the orb of light wobble across the wasteland. Moments later it disappeared into the darkness.

"What—was—*that*?" Liam asked.

Grace bit her fingernails. Her eyes darted from Liam to the pylon, and then back to Liam.

"I'm not sure if I wanna know," she said.

CHAPTER
3

When Grace and Liam finally set foot back in New Asheville, the sun was just peeking over the horizon.

"School in two hours," Grace grumbled.

Liam yawned. "Not even worth going to sleep now."

"Then let's do some research on floating green ghosts," Grace said with a smirk.

Liam raised an eyebrow. "Library?"

Grace nodded.

The library, like everything else in New Asheville, was white, shiny, and simple in design. Grace liked to say that the city's architects must've been afraid to put any creativity into the place for fear it'd just go the way of Old Asheville someday.

Liam admired the clean, modern building, its roof lined with solar panels. He felt comforted looking at it. The simplicity of the design provided a stark contrast to the wasteland surrounding the town.

Liam rubbed his eyes and said, "I think the people who built this place designed it to make people feel safe."

Grace furrowed her brow. "I don't feel that way when I look at it. I feel on edge and anxious."

Liam pulled open the heavy glass door and gave an exaggerated bow. "Cynical philosophers first!" he said mockingly.

Grace chuckled. "Okay, okay, I'll try to lighten up a bit."

The two of them made their way to a data terminal. The library had just opened. It was nearly empty. Grace sat down in a chair at the terminal, and Liam pulled another one up next to her. The terminal was little more than a touch screen set atop a white pole in the floor. Liam

thought it looked like a friendly robot's head
and neck.

Grace immediately starting typing
keywords into the local database: *green; light; ghost;
RadZone; sightings; pylon.* Search results populated
the screen, including forum discussions, news
reports, and scientific documents. Grace started
with the news reports.

"Asheville citizens report seeing strange
green lights in RadZone sectors," she read aloud.

"Score," Liam said.

Grace quickly scanned the rest of the
article. "Yeah, but it doesn't help us much.
The story just seems to summarize other
people's accounts."

"Any of them still living here?" Liam asked.

"None of the names ring a bell," she said.
She grinned mischievously. "Maybe the green
ghost came to get them."

"Ha," Liam said flatly. "What else
is there?"

Grace scanned a few of the forum results
and snickered. "This is hilarious. They're
all talking about radiated nuke-zombies and

something called the 'will-o'-the-wisp.' How old are these people—twelve?"

"When I was a kid, my dad joked he'd give my dinner to the nuke-zombies living in the RadZones if I didn't finish," Liam said, chuckling. "It never worked."

Grace stared blankly. "Yeah. Ridiculous."

"What's the 'will-o'-the-wisp' stuff about?" Liam asked.

Grace brought up a new search. "Also known as corpselights or fools' fire, will-o'-the-wisps are a light-based phenomenon reported across the world as unexplainable floating lights. The flickering lights are said to draw travelers away from safe paths to treacherous ground, such as marshes, bogs, or other wastelands—often to their deaths."

"Our light didn't flicker," Liam said.

Grace nodded. "Either way, good thing we didn't follow it into the RadZone, huh? It definitely would have gotten us killed."

"No kidding," Liam agreed.

Then they went silent. Neither of them wanted to say it, but the description felt rather ominous after last week's most recent incident. Some scientist had just walked straight into the irradiated zone as though he'd been beckoned to his own death.

Liam cleared his throat and stood. "We're gonna be late for school."

Grace's face suddenly brightened. "Oh! I'm supposed to do story time for the kindergartners today."

She stood up so fast her chair tipped over. Liam righted it and smiled. Grace loved to scare little kids. It was her way of bonding with them.

"At least you'll have some good nightmare fuel for your story after tonight."

Grace's face lit up. "Ohhhh, yeah. This'll be good. You should come and watch."

"Count me in."

Together they left the library.

CHAPTER
4

A row of expectant and horrified little faces stared up at Grace, an LED illuminating her face from below.

"The little girl was afraid, but she kept very still. She didn't breathe, and she didn't run despite her fear," Grace said, her voice growing deeper and lower. "She felt like time had stopped, but her heartbeat was racing." Grace thumped her hand on her chest to mimic a beating heart. "But after a few minutes, she worked up the courage to peek over the wall . . . "

Grace paused. "AND THEN THE NUKE-ZOMBIE GRABBED HER!" she howled, flicking the LED light off and on.

Screams of glee and terror filled the classroom. The kindergartners ran around like terrified baby chicks as their teacher tried to calm them down. Grace cackled.

"I can't believe they let you do story time," Liam said, opening the shades. He'd been leaning against a wall in the back of the classroom, delighting in Grace's tale. "Those kids will have some tired parents come tomorrow morning."

Grace grinned. "It's good for them."

"The parents or the kids?" Liam asked.

The kids began to tug at Grace's arms and legs, begging for one more story. Grace looked down at the kids, then back at Liam. Her face looked drawn and pale. "Both," she said. She turned back to the kindergartners and put on her biggest, warmest smile. "Sorry, kids, but I have to go back to my class now."

The kids pouted as Grace waved good-bye. She thought her stories prepared the kids for the everyday terrors of life living in a city bordered by radiation. Liam thought they were just a good distraction.

There were about two hundred people living in New Asheville. Most of the adults were nuclear engineers, scientists, or doctors. Most of the kids were just victims of parents with important jobs and unfortunate circumstances. A few years back, when the radiation spilled over into the only safe entrance point to the city, everyone there became trapped. Even modern aerial vehicles couldn't safely get to them—the few that still existed, anyway.

Liam sighed. "I don't know how I'm gonna stay awake in our NukeSci class."

"Really?" Grace said. "I don't know how I'm gonna get to sleep after what we saw last night."

Liam stopped her in the hallway. "Should we tell somebody? Your dad, maybe?"

"No way. I don't wanna be known as the crazy kid here."

"Too late for that," Liam joked.

Smart remarks normally earned Liam a chuckle and an elbow in the ribs, but this time Grace just walked on, opened the door to their classroom, and slipped inside.

Liam followed. "I was just kidding," he said—not quite loud enough for Grace to hear.

Mr. Sievert was lecturing as the two of them took their seats. He was explaining the Standard Precautionary Procedure Regarding Radioactive Zones.

As if we need more warnings, Liam thought.

Every school year, they had to go over all the dreadful history of their town and study safety precautions. Ashevillians lived in this terrible place day in and day out, never completely free from the knowledge that they could be killed within minutes if they dared stray beyond the red holographic barriers and into the town's borderlands. Fear loomed over the town, like a cloud of deadly radiation. At no point was the threat far from anyone's mind.

Grace's in particular, Liam thought, looking at her. Her face was buried in her palms as if she were thinking about something.

Liam let out a heavy sigh. *We're going out again tonight,* he realized.

Grace met his eyes and gave him a little smile.

CHAPTER
5

Grace looked frazzled. They'd managed to sneak in a few hours of sleep between the end of school and dusk, but Liam had a feeling that something more than restlessness was under her skin. Yet here they were, back near the basement entrance to the Victorian house, waiting for the green light to appear again.

What exactly are we going to do if it does? Liam thought. *Follow it into the RadZone?*

It just made no sense. Sure, Liam wanted answers—maybe just as much as Grace did. But he couldn't imagine a floating light could provide any.

Grace hadn't moved an inch since they'd arrived at the house. She crouched behind the concrete wall bordering the stairs, her eyes fixed on some point off in the distance.

Liam shifted from one foot to the other, observing his friend for signs of a meltdown. As it turns out, living in an area surrounded by death had a tendency to make people feel suicidal. Who knew? The last guy to off himself had left a note simply stating he was "going home." But Grace wouldn't do something like that, he was sure.

"You aren't going crazy on me, are you, Grace?" Liam asked quietly.

"I'm fine, Liam," she said, her lips barely moving.

Liam blinked his eyes hard for a second to give them a break. When he opened them, he saw something in the distance. Something green. He blinked again. Still there. He rubbed his eyes. The light was closer.

"Do you see it?" Liam whispered.

"Yes."

Liam lowered himself behind the concrete ledge and peered over it, his eyes as big as twin moons. In silence, they watched the green light move closer and closer. A figure began to take shape next to the light.

"No way," Liam whispered. "Is that a man? There's just no way. He'd be puking blood by now."

"Shh!" Grace whispered.

The thing left the irradiated zone by passing through the barrier. No alarms sounded. *Why aren't the alarms sounding?* Liam thought. *They react to the human heartbeat . . .*

Whatever it was, it headed straight toward them.

"Duck," Liam said. "*Now.*"

"Why?" Grace asked. "It looks human."

"If that thing were human," Liam said, "it'd be dead. *Get. Down.*"

The two of them pressed their backs against the concrete wall. Seconds passed, each one rendering an eternity of anxiety. Liam's neck hairs were on high alert; his flesh prickled with goose bumps.

Then the pale man, if you could call it a man, ambled past them. A strange lantern in his left hand cast a sickly glow on his shriveled skin. He held a small electronic device in his other hand. His milky eyes were sunken and gray. His mouth was drawn; his lips were thin. What little hair he had on his scalp was patchy and unkempt. Liam thought he looked like an unwrapped mummy wearing synthetic white pants and shirt.

When he had passed out of sight, Grace's and Liam's eyes reflected each other's shock.

"We have to follow him," Grace said.

"Are you insane?" Liam hissed. "That thing is a freakin' nuke-zombie!"

Grace peered over the edge of the concrete wall they hid behind. Liam poked his head up and saw the pale man heading toward an old, dilapidated house with a garage attached. The man looked left, then right, and then inserted a key into a lock on the side of the garage.

Liam ducked down again, but Grace stood and moved to follow.

Liam grabbed her by the wrist. "Grace, stop! Whatever that thing is, it's not *alive*. For all we know, the urban legends of those meltdowners coming back as zombies are true!"

Grace jerked her hand away. "There's no such thing as zombies," she said, and then ran after the pale figure.

Liam closed his eyes. For a moment he sat there, paralyzed by a surreal mix of terror and anxiety. He forced himself to slowly breathe in and out. Then he opened his eyes and stood. He grabbed a metal rod from a pile of rubble, clenched his teeth, and ran after his friend.

CHAPTER
6

The two-foot-long metal bar in Liam's fist pumped up and down as he ran. In the distance, Grace had approached the pale man. He was staring at her with wide eyes while she gestured with her hands.

The man raised his lantern to shoulder height. *It's some sort of weapon!* Liam thought. His legs pumped harder, adrenaline forcing his limbs to move faster than he'd thought possible.

Liam screamed, "Don't hurt her!" Three seconds later, he was on top of the pale figure with the rod raised over his head.

"Stop it, Liam!" Grace cried.

Her words snapped Liam to attention. He locked eyes with her, his hands still tight around the rod. The pale thing in front of him watched but said nothing.

"Please, stop, Liam," Grace said softly. She placed both hands on his shoulders. "He's friendly, I promise," she added.

Liam reluctantly lowered his weapon.

"What *are* you?" he challenged the man.

Grace turned to face the pale man. "Don't mind him. He's just tense. We're all tense. You know, on account of the radiation—and, well, everything."

The man nodded. "Understandable," he said in a raspy voice. "So you know about the encroaching radiation?"

Liam's and Grace's mouths dropped open. Liam had been waiting for the man to speak, but actually hearing words come from seemingly dead lips was unsettling.

"Yeah, we do," Liam said, recovering his courage. "But how do *you* know about it?"

The pale man gazed at Liam, then at Grace, and then back to Liam. "Follow me."

He opened the garage's side door and entered, his lantern illuminating the way.

Grace glanced at Liam. "Is this really happening?"

Liam's jaw tightened. "Yeah—and I don't trust that *thing*."

Grace frowned. "He's obviously human, and he seems harmless." She looked down at the rod in Liam's hand. "Leave that here."

Liam tightened his grip on the weapon and shook his head no. Grace sighed. With that, they entered the garage and followed the man into the house. In the hardwood floor of the kitchen, a five-by-five trapdoor had been propped up, revealing what looked like a wine cellar below. Intense white light radiated upward, bathing the dusty kitchen in an artificial glow.

"How does he have power here?" Liam asked.

Grace shrugged. "Let's find out."

CHAPTER
7

Liam shielded his eyes with his free hand.

"Welcome to my lab," the pale man said, his voice coarse. "My name is Dr. Litchfield."

Grace walked into the center of the room and twirled slowly to take everything in.

Liam lowered his hand as his eyes adjusted to the brightness. The entire ceiling was layered with square bricks of lights. His aching eyes boggled at countless strange devices set atop workbenches lining the walls of the lab.

"How did you do all this?" Grace asked, her eyes as wide as her smile.

"I had lots of . . . time," Litchfield said, his voice strained but clearer now.

"What does that mean?" Liam asked. He carefully skirted around a cylindrical object with a tube leading to what looked like a gas mask.

Litchfield lifted his lantern, set it on the table, and placed a hand protectively on the object, much like a father laying a hand on his child's head.

"Forgive me if my speech is . . . strange. I haven't spoken much."

He's avoiding the question, Liam decided.

"This is creepy," he said out loud. He looked into Litchfield's milky-white eyes. "I don't trust you. What is going on down here? Who are you?" Liam's hands tightened around the rod as his eyes focused on the lantern. "And what is *that?* Some kind of weapon?"

Litchfield placed both hands on the lantern.

"This?" he asked. "It's not a weapon. I call it the Litch-Cell."

Liam narrowed his eyes. "Litch-Cell?" he repeated.

"Not the most creative name, I know," Litchfield said. "But it fits."

Grace tilted her head. "Cell? As in a battery cell?"

Litchfield nodded. "And somewhat of a holding cell. It contains a part of me."

Liam rubbed his eyes, frustration contorting his face. "And that would be . . . ?"

Litchfield looked Liam in the eyes. "I suppose you call it my soul."

Liam stared blankly at Litchfield. "I don't believe for a second that the ball of light in there is your soul. I don't believe in souls or magic or any of that."

Litchfield glanced down in thought. A few long moments later, he looked past both Liam and Grace at nothing in particular and said, "Perhaps what we call 'magic' is just what science yet lacks the ability to define."

Grace smiled. Litchfield nodded at her. "You agree?" he asked.

Grace shrugged. "I dunno. To be honest, I don't really know what to think about any of this right now." She glanced at the lantern. "But if that *is* your soul in that cell, *how* did you manage to put it in there, and *why*?"

Litchfield nodded. "Short or long version?"

"Short," Liam snapped.

"Long," Grace said.

Liam tossed the metal rod he'd been carrying onto a nearby table and sat down against the wall. He lifted the hood of his sweatshirt and pulled it over his eyes. "Wake me up when he gets to the part about why he's a nuke-zombie."

Grace frowned. "Why are you being such a jerk?"

Liam grunted.

"It's understandable," Litchfield said. "I know what I look like. And—Liam, is it?—is right, in a way. Several others thought I was a zombie the first time they saw me, too."

Grace leaned back a little. Liam peered through his hood.

Litchfield leaned back against the wall. "What's more, I don't need to eat. I don't need to sleep. For decades I've been alone, buried in my research, trying to find answers." He placed his hand on his Litch-Cell again. "If it weren't for this device, I'd have died many years ago."

43

Grace sat down—or more accurately, fell into a chair. "This is all a bit much."

Litchfield nodded. "I know it's hard to believe, and I know you have all sorts of questions. I was initially skeptical of you two, as well, but the fact that you haven't reacted like the others is encouraging."

Grace leaned forward. "The others?" she asked. Her eyes went wide. "So *you* were the cause behind those supposed zombie sightings?"

Litchfield frowned. "I've tried to approach people in the past," he said. "Each time I did, they either tried to harm me or ran away screaming. The fact that you didn't attack me or flee tells me everything I need to know."

Grace tilted her head. "And what is that?"

Litchfield shrugged. "That you might help me."

Liam leaned forward, placing his elbows on his knees. "To be fair, I almost hit you—and I still might."

Litchfield nodded soberly. "Fair enough," he said.

The conversation had hit a stalemate. The opportunities for doubt, questions, and wonder were endless, and no one knew which subject to tackle first.

"I'm sure you have many questions," Litchfield said. "But perhaps we should all sleep on it and finish our discussion tomorrow."

Liam tilted his head. "But you don't sleep, you said."

Litchfield hesitated. "No," he admitted. "In my case, it's only a figure of speech. I will continue my work throughout the night."

CHAPTER
8

Liam waved good-bye to Grace as he walked away from her house. She smiled, waved back, and then closed the door.

Liam was wired. His heart was still racing. They'd left Litchfield's lab shortly after his suggestion that they sleep on things and pick up the discussion tomorrow. On their way home, Grace seemed calmer than she had in a while. Meanwhile Liam was a wreck. He'd told her he would go home, get some sleep, and meet her the next morning. But thoughts were whirling around in his head. It was hard enough to believe that someone like Litchfield existed, let alone to trust him.

Liam got home, sneaked upstairs, and crawled into his bed with his clothes still on.

He closed his eyes and tried to let himself fall into unconsciousness.

Soaked in adrenaline, he realized there was no way he'd be getting any sleep that night. So he got up, went downstairs, walked outside—and just kept walking, heading nowhere in particular.

Soon he found himself on the border of Old Asheville. His feet carried him back to the old Victorian. Liam sat on the floor of the entryway, staring into the black space that had opened up beneath their feet. All he could see below was darkness, framed by the rotted-away remains of the wooden staircase.

Liam found himself staring into that deep darkness below, wondering what was down there—despite knowing full well it was just an empty basement. Still, he couldn't quite get himself to aim his LED below and reveal it. He wasn't sure why he couldn't do it—and that fact agitated him even farther. His legs grew restless, feeling like they'd walk away on their own if Liam didn't hold them down.

Liam gritted his teeth. He aimed his LED down into the basement and peered over the edge.

Countless pale figures with dead eyes stared up at him.

Liam screamed.

✦ ✦ ✦ ✦ ✦

Liam jumped out of bed so fast that he knocked over his bedside table and fell hard on his side. He skittered across the floor until his back was pressed against the wall. Only then did he realize he'd been dreaming.

Light filtered in through his window, casting a glow on the beads of sweat that had gathered on his forehead. He closed his eyes and leaned his head back, trying to get his breathing under control, berating himself for acting like a three-year-old who'd just had his first nightmare.

"What's wrong?"

Liam's eyes opened. His father was looking down at him.

"What?" Liam said, bewildered. He hadn't even heard his father enter the room.

His dad's hands were on his hips, and he had that slightly disappointed parental look on his face. "You're acting strangely lately," he said. "It's not because of that last death? I don't understand, either, why people decide one day to just walk into the RadZone."

Liam rolled his eyes. "No, dad, it's not that."

"Then what is it?"

Liam got up and put on his best fake smile. "I dreamed I was being chased by zombies," he said, looking up to meet his dad's gaze.

His dad smiled wryly. With a nod, he walked toward the door, seemingly satisfied that his son wasn't on drugs. Over his shoulder he added, "I never should have told you kids those zombie stories when you were younger."

Liam forced a chuckle, thinking back on Grace's story time yesterday.

CHAPTER
9

Liam waited for his dad to leave the house before he left his room. It was Saturday, but Liam didn't want to have to lie to his dad about where he was going. He jumped into his shoes and ran out the front door. Grace had told him to meet her at the old Victorian in about five minutes from now. Nightmares aside, Liam was glad to have overslept a bit. He still felt that ache in the back of his head where it had smacked against the concrete basement floor, but he at least was feeling more rested. He decided to turn a fifteen-minute walk into a five-minute jog.

Four minutes and thirty seconds later, Grace waved at him. He came to a stop next to her and bent over with his hands on his knees.

"Why were you running?" she asked.

Liam wiped the sweat from his brow. "I dunno."

Grace gave him a long look and then stood. "Ready?" she asked.

Liam straightened himself up. "Sure," he lied.

✦ ✦ ✦ ✦ ✦

They found Litchfield sitting in a chair in a corner, staring at the wall. He looked up when they entered.

"Hello," he said. "How'd you sleep?"

Liam raised an eyebrow. "About as well as you, it seems," he said.

Litchfield nodded. "Understandable."

Grace got right to the point, as usual. "Let's say we believe your story," she said. "Then all I need to know is: Who are you *really*—and what are you doing down here?"

Litchfield stood slowly. Liam could hear his joints creak as he straightened up.

"Short version," Litchfield said, nodding at Liam. "I used to be a scientist—a nuclear scientist, to be precise. I worked on the Kerrigan Reactor. As luck would have it, I was in one of the safe zones when the reactor went critical. I was the only one working at the power plant to survive. Everyone I knew died in the ensuing explosion and fallout. I helped create the RadZone barriers once the dust had settled. But in my spare time, in secret, I designed and created this." He gestured at the Litch-Cell. "It holds the essential energy of my body in radiation-proof housing. It allows me to enter the irradiated zones."

Liam furrowed his brow in doubt. "That'd make you . . . what . . . 150 years old?"

Litchfield chuckled dryly. "About that. Anyhow, I took it upon myself to try to fix the reactor. But as you both know, the reactor is leaking again. Radiation is being released at alarmingly high levels. It's only a matter of time until the core splits wide open and the barriers fail, exposing New Asheville to deadly radiation."

Grace hung her head. "It's even worse than Dad said."

Litchfield observed the silence for a moment. "But fear not. Containing the radiation wasn't my primary mission—it was just a way to buy me more time."

"Time for what?" Liam asked.

"To build this," Litchfield said, pressing a long, slender finger into a square-shaped hole in the wall.

Rotors turned inside the walls. Liam jumped back in alarm.

Grace and Liam watched wide-eyed as a panel of the wall began to slide open, revealing a secret compartment bathed in eerie green light.

In the compartment was a machine about the size of a small car. In the center of it was a clear glass cylinder containing a ball that emanated green, strobing light. The green orb bobbed up and down slowly, suspended in liquid. In the bottom-center of the machine was a gap that looked about the same size as Litchfield's cell.

Grace covered her mouth with one hand and pointed at the device with the other. "Is that—is that a . . ."

Litchfield nodded. "It's a Kerrigan Reactor."

Grace leaped up from her chair and faced Litchfield. "Are you insane? That's the thing that created this mess, and you're building a new one?"

Despite her fury, Grace was still as stone except for a slight twitch in her left eye—the twitch Liam worried about. It was the one sign that indicated Grace wasn't as calm as she seemed.

Liam moved closer to Litchfield. He clenched his fists, ready for whatever would come next.

Litchfield didn't move. He just met Grace's glare with his milky gaze. But Liam noticed something else in the man's eyes: perhaps sadness or weariness. *No, not either of those,* Liam thought. *Something else.*

"You're right to be angry," Litchfield said, turning to face the machine. Green light reached around him like a spectral hand and cast a shadow on the opposite wall. "The reactor caused all this madness, yes. It was flawed, terribly flawed. But even so, it was a brilliant design. Over the years, I figured out what went wrong. And when I'm done with this version, it'll be safe." Litchfield placed his hands on the cylinder. "And what's more, it'll be self-sufficient—and will produce enough energy to power the entire world."

Neither Liam nor Grace made any discernible reaction. They were stunned, in shock, and fearful of what might happen if Litchfield's plans came to fruition.

Litchfield's face grew serious. He placed his hands on his hips. "But I've saved the best part for last," he said. "This device will also be able to absorb harmful radiation and recycle it as usable energy."

Even Liam, in all his skepticism, hadn't expected Litchfield to say such an outlandish thing. The scope of the situation felt too big, too vast to process. Liam rubbed the back of his head to ease the metallic pinching in the base of his brain. "This is crazy."

Grace caught Liam's eyes and nodded. "But if he's telling the truth, this thing could save the world."

Liam shrugged. "Or it could destroy what's left of it."

Litchfield nodded. "You're both right. But you should ask yourselves why a man would put himself through more than a century of solitude, dedicating every moment of his nonlife to creating something only for the purpose of destroying it all. Seems like a lot of work to put into destruction, don't you think?" He entered the main section of his lab again. "It has been my many-lives' mission to fix what was done here—what led to the worldwide energy shortage and the deaths of countless innocents. The chain reaction of events that brought us to the present doesn't have to end in extinction. At least, not for Asheville."

"Well, I don't trust you one bit," Liam said. Grace's tired eyes pleaded with him. "But I trust Grace's judgment."

Grace smiled at Liam in that special way. The way that made him feel that she saw him as no one else did—past the surface and into his soul. He turned to hide the blush spreading up his neck. "But if this guy tries to eat your brains, I'm totally gonna go Kerrigan on him."

Litchfield's face changed, and Liam thought he almost smiled, but it was nearly impossible to tell since his lips hardly moved.

"As I think I mentioned before, I no longer need to eat," the scientist quipped.

Liam laughed in spite of himself. Grace let out a sigh of relief, probably because Liam was relaxing a little.

Litchfield stuffed his spindly fingers into the pockets of his pants and hung his head. "Anyway, I'm glad you two came along. For years I've sought help to no avail. Now here you two sit. Will you help me save Asheville?"

Grace smiled softly at Liam. In that moment, he would've agreed to anything. "Count us in," Liam said.

Litchfield smiled broadly, revealing a complete absence of teeth.

"So, how can we help?" Grace chirped. Liam couldn't help but smile at her excitement. *Even if it is foolish,* he thought.

"I need a data terminal from the library," Litchfield said flatly. "Not the wiring—I have plenty of that lying around. Just the terminal itself."

"Why?" Grace asked.

Litchfield crossed his thin arms. "It's . . . hard to explain."

Liam rolled his eyes. "Right, sure," he said. "We'll just go trash the library and steal a terminal for you on faith."

"Not faith. *Hope*," Litchfield said. "Hope that Asheville isn't doomed."

"We'll do it tonight," Grace said.

CHAPTER
10

Previously, Liam had felt safe and calm in the sterile simplicity of the library. But tonight, as he gazed at the strangely glowing data terminal sprouting from the floor, the place seemed more like a poorly lit hospital where sick robots went to die. He wondered what had changed in him since their visit earlier in the week.

Anger began to bubble in his breast. "I don't like this place," he said.

Grace faced the terminal. "Me either. So let's get this over with, okay?"

Liam placed his hands around the neck of the terminal and turned it counterclockwise. The outer casing clicked and separated into two halves.

Grace eyed the wires that now lay exposed. She traced them up to the terminal itself and pawed at the clasp beneath. A few moments later she found a release switch.

"You're up, muscles," she said.

Liam hesitated. *Why am I doing this?* he wondered. He'd thought it over on the walk to the library, but it still seemed like he didn't have a choice. He'd been infected by Grace's hope, or something.

It made him feel weak. And angry.

He pulled on the terminal, attempting to free it from the wires. It didn't budge. He pulled harder.

"Hold on; it's caught on something," Grace said. She lay on her back and shined her LED under the terminal. She reached into her pocket and produced a knife, opened it, and pressed it against something under the terminal.

"You always carry a knife around?" he asked.

Grace shifted her body to put more pressure on the blade. "No."

60

"Why today?" he asked, shifting his body to rest the terminal's weight on his hip.

"Not telling."

Liam heard a *snap* as the first clasp was cut.

"Why?" he asked as Grace set to work on cutting the second clasp.

"You'll laugh at me," she said quietly.

Their eyes met. "I won't."

Grace kept her gaze on him. He could tell she knew he was telling the truth.

Grace continued to cut at the clasp. She pushed against the floor and arched her back. *Snap!* The terminal came free.

"I felt safer with it on me . . . after seeing Litchfield's light," she mumbled.

Liam chuckled.

Grace got to her feet and glared at Liam. "You said you wouldn't laugh at me!"

Liam smiled. "I'm not. It's just that I get it. Fear makes us do funny things." He paused. "Like the way your eye twitches when you're nervous," he added quietly.

Grace's glare turned soft and vulnerable. She stared down at her feet. "You notice that?"

Liam nodded. "You're one of the calmest people I know," he said. "But things still get to you. You're not a zombie."

Grace smiled. "Litchfield's not one, either."

"I know," Liam said. "I saw something in his eyes. Some part of him is still human." *I'm just not sure it's the good part*, he wanted to add but didn't.

Grace stared down at her feet. "You ready?"

"Let's do this," Liam said. Carefully, he lifted the terminal. It was surprisingly heavy, but not too heavy for him to heft. As the head came off the neck, a small connector pin snapped free—and a deafening alarm rang out.

Their eyes met. Then they ran.

CHAPTER
11

Liam and Grace panted together behind a broken-down old house. They had been ducking and weaving through the shadows to get here. And they both needed a moment to catch their breaths.

Off in the distance, they could hear sirens and see flashes of light from New Ashville's security forces. Grace had worried about getting caught on a security camera, which is why they took the roundabout way to get here.

Liam took a deep breath and then picked the data terminal back up. His arms burned from its weight. Together, they walked through the night, with Grace leading the way. After a few minutes, she grabbed Liam's arm and pointed.

"Look!" she said.

Huge plumes of mossy green and neon blue light threaded mistily against the night sky like some sort of nuclear aurora borealis. Grace and Liam stared up in silence. In that moment, both forgot all about death, radiation, and Litchfield.

The initial awe and wonder soon gave way to bitter resignation. Grace put her hands on her hips. "Ironic, isn't it? Something so beautiful is a reminder that things are getting worse."

Liam nodded soberly but kept his gaze skyward. The melding lights were the result of enormous chemical reactions occurring within the pylons of the RadZone barrier. Ions were being shed from the barrier as it was hit by encroaching radiation. In other words, whenever the light show made an appearance, it meant the pylons were losing the battle against the radiation.

Time was running out. Who knew how long they had left? It made Liam feel bitter; Grace had to know the way he felt about her by now. But what was the point? *There's no room for sappy stuff when everything around you is dying*, he thought. He clenched his teeth.

Grace observed the series of emotions unfolding on Liam's face. "What are you thinking?" she asked softly.

"Nothing," Liam said. Caught off guard, he'd spoken more harshly than he intended. "It's nothing," he repeated, more gently. "It's just I don't know if helping Litchfield is the right thing to do. Are you sure you don't want to ask your dad about this?"

Grace frowned. "He wouldn't believe me. He's so worried about the radiation that he barely listens to me."

Liam awkwardly placed his hand on her shoulder.

Grace sighed. "It's not like helping Litchfield could make things any worse."

Liam wasn't sure if that was true, but he smiled anyway. "Yeah," he said.

With one last glance at the ominous display playing out in the sky overhead, Liam followed Grace, his eyes fixed on the point where her feet met the earth.

CHAPTER
12

Together they walked into Litchfield's house. To their surprise, the door leading downstairs was still open. Light—white and green—radiated out.

After entering the lab, they saw him once again sitting in a chair facing the wall. He didn't acknowledge them.

"Um," Grace said. "Hello?"

"Oh. Sorry. I didn't hear you come in," Litchfield said.

Liam narrowed his eyes. "What's with the staring-at-the-wall thing?"

Litchfield stood and faced them. It seemed to take a few minutes for him to collect his thoughts. "It's how I think. I clear my mind,

stare at the wall, and work out problems
and calculations."

"Sounds like meditation," Grace said.

Litchfield half-grinned. "Maybe."

Liam gently set the terminal on one of the
few empty spaces on a workbench.

"Good, good!" Litchfield said, rubbing his
hands together. "You'll have to leave me with
the device now—I have to seal myself inside the
compartment when I'm working on the reactor.
Radiation and all that. You can wait out here,
though it will probably be a while. Better to
come back tomorrow night."

Litchfield regarded the two of them with
a blank expression. Usually Liam was good at
reading people, but because most of Litchfield's
facial tissue had hardened, there weren't any
micro-expressions for him to read. Litchfield's
body language, though, spoke volumes. Litchfield
had positioned himself behind a workbench,
as though distancing or protecting himself
from them.

Liam was certain of it now. "You're hiding
something," he said.

"Liam," Grace said, "Just let it go, okay?"

Liam wrinkled his nose. "How do we know he's not exposing us to radiation right now?"

"It's okay, Liam," Grace said. "I've been checking the radiation levels with my LED's RadCounter since we first met him. It's why he raised his lantern when I first made contact—so I could get a reading on it."

Liam's stomach sank. "Why didn't you tell me?"

Grace shrugged. "I don't know. I didn't think it was necessary."

Normally Liam would've shrugged it off, but after the sleep deprivation, stealing a library terminal, and then fleeing the scene of a crime, he didn't have the energy to fight back the anger.

"Whatever," he said. "I'll leave you two to your secrets."

"Wait," Grace said, but Liam waved a hand over his shoulder and kept walking.

After he'd gone, Grace plunked down into a chair.

Litchfield tilted his head. "Are you two sweethearts?"

Grace's head lurched back. "What? No way. No." She slumped farther into her chair. "I mean, I don't know. He's kind of overprotective, I guess." Her eyes met Litchfield's; then she stared at her feet. "Never mind."

Litchfield crossed his arms. "Boys are tricky," he said. Grace looked up at him without raising her head. "See, boys are only protective of what they care about. That's how they show affection. And I can tell your . . . friend, Liam, is afraid. And he's angry."

Grace tilted her head. "Angry about what?"

Litchfield shrugged. "Life, maybe? Everyone reacts to stress in different ways. And you two—well, everyone in New Asheville— must be under an inordinate amount of stress."

Grace laughed. "You can say that again. Just last week, another person had a meltdown. Walked right into the irradiated zone and kept walking until he practically melted. It's . . . it's so . . ."

"Terrible," Litchfield said. "But like I said, people react to stress in different ways."

Grace looked up at Litchfield with genuine doubt. This time he didn't look away. "Oh, yeah?" she asked. "Then what about you? You don't seem stressed. Not one bit."

Litchfield nodded. "Losing your soul will do that to you," he said. "And I've been alone for decades. Time erodes. It wears things down. Be it rock, metal, or emotions."

Grace frowned. "I'll admit, that's a good answer. But it also sounds kind of prepared."

"Most of what I say is prepared," Litchfield admitted. "I've had many years to think about it. Between the time alone and my condition, I'm afraid I lack the capacity to be surprised anymore."

Grace's shoulders slumped. "Sorry. I forget what you've been through."

Litchfield waved dismissively. "No need to apologize."

Grace stood and leaned against the wall. "I am curious, though, about your soul. What is it? It bothers me that you think you've taken something that's supposed to be beyond the physical world and trapped it in that cell of yours. Kind of contradictory, don't you think?"

Litchfield uncrossed his arms and sat down. "This is a conversation worth having," he said. "The soul, what it means—what it actually *is* . . ." He stood again. Grace could tell he was getting restless. "I have to admit to you that I don't have all the answers. My original goal was to contain all the electrons in my body in the Litch-Cell. When I finally succeeded, everything felt . . . different. Kind of turned down, like the volume on a radio."

Grace said nothing, waiting for a better answer.

Litchfield paced around the room. "Years and years of thinking have led me to believe that humans only perceive a small part of reality. We are limited by our senses. With mine turned down, I was able to focus on specifics much more easily. Emotions didn't get in the way. The progress I made in my research was astounding, if I do say so myself." He stopped pacing and faced Grace. "But I felt every minute of it. Every second. Time never sped up. In fact, some days, it seemed to drag on forever—and I was glad of feeling detached from everything. Otherwise it would've been unbearable."

Grace slowly stood and walked closer to Litchfield. "You're avoiding the question," she said. "What is a soul? And why do you feel so detached without it?"

Litchfield shrugged. "Smart girl. Honestly, I just don't know. Why did I feel detached? At first, I assumed it was chemical or biological—a result of low serotonin or another neurotransmitter in the brain—but I ran tests. Nothing quite explains it."

Grace looked into Litchfield's milky-white eyes. She wondered if he even had the capacity to cry. If anything could move him to tears. "So, magic, then?" she said, smiling—and letting him off the hook.

Litchfield smiled a real smile once again. "I can't explain it," he admitted. "I should've just said that in the first place, huh?"

Grace smirked. "I think you'll eventually figure it out."

And in that moment, Grace saw something change in Litchfield. His skin remained unmoved, but something beneath it, maybe muscle, maybe bone, maybe something else— something smoothed over and gave him an expression of peace.

He glanced out the window. "Thank you for talking with me, Grace," he said. "Perhaps I was wrong to say I'd prepared myself for every kind of conversation." He turned and picked up the data terminal with surprising ease and headed toward his smaller room. "I must be going now. My work is not yet done." He turned back. "But please, return at your earliest convenience. I do enjoy your brains." He turned, sort-of-smiled, and closed the door behind him.

Grace grinned.

On her way home, she stopped at the Victorian mansion that had almost swallowed her and Liam up. She entered the living area and plucked a single book from the shelf. She tucked it under her arm and headed to Liam's house.

CHAPTER
13

Liam couldn't sleep. Even after wrapping his head in his pillow and putting another one over his head, he just couldn't keep the world out. His thoughts kept wandering back to Grace and why he'd gotten so angry.

He threw a pillow across the room and sat up. That's when he realized the truth: he was jealous. He'd been trying so hard for so long to get her to cheer up, and some glorified science-zombie with a ticking time bomb put her at ease.

He rubbed the bridge of his nose and sighed. Then he broke into laughter. "You're such an idiot, Liam," he said to himself. "She's handling the stress better than you are. That's all."

Liam leaped out of bed, snaked his legs into a pair of ratty jeans, and then crammed his feet into his shoes. "Either way, you gotta go apologize to her."

He ran downstairs, grabbed his LED, and reached for the door. Just then, a knock sounded.

Liam slowly opened the door to reveal Grace.

"Hey," she said uncertainly.

"Hey," Liam said. "Uh," panicking over what to say, he pointed at the object she held under an arm. "What's that?"

"A book for Litchfield," she said.

Liam nodded. "Ah."

"We talked a while after you left," Grace said. "He's the real deal. The reactor model he's working on is basically the same thing my dad is in the early planning stages of." She shifted her weight to one foot. "And I saw something in his eyes, Liam—just like you said. I agree that there's something he's not telling us, but I don't think it's something bad."

Liam's shoulders went slack. "I don't know about that."

Grace's eyes met his. "Please trust me, Liam?"

"Don't worry," he said. "You know I've got your back—no matter what. And I trust you on this." He stepped out to the porch and closed the door most of the way behind him. "I'm sorry for snapping at you earlier. It's just that—"

Grace smiled at him. "There's nothing to apologize for. You're the only reason I haven't completely lost my mind the last few months."

A goofy grin popped up on Liam's face. "Ditto," he said.

CHAPTER
14

The next evening, sneaking out was a little more difficult. New Asheville was under curfew after the theft of the library's data terminal. Thankfully, the security cameras around town didn't get a good view of Liam or Grace. But security forces knew it was a pair of thieves that had committed the crime. So that night, Liam and Grace had to sneak to Litchfield's lab separately.

Several times along the way, Liam had to duck for cover as a security vehicle cruised by. When he finally arrived at the lab, and Grace wasn't there, he was worried that it was something more than just her tendency to be late. But a few minutes later, she burst out of the night, breathing heavily. Liam ran over to her.

"Were you being chased?" he asked.

She nodded as she bent over and tried to catch her breath.

"Did anyone follow you here?"

She shook her head. "No, I . . . led them . . . away . . . That's why . . . it took me so long . . . to get here."

She inhaled deeply and stood up straight.

"Let's go," she said.

As they entered the lab, Litchfield wasn't sitting and staring—he was tinkering with his Litch-Cell.

"I brought you something," Grace said, extending a leather-bound book.

Litchfield looked up. He took the book with both hands and dusted off the cover. "*The Collected Stories of Arthur C. Clarke*," he read aloud. "Was it that obvious I'm a fan?"

"The whole thing about magic and science tipped me off," Grace said with a knowing smile.

Litchfield nodded. He set the book down ceremoniously in the center of an otherwise relatively empty table. Then he turned to face

Liam and Grace. "If anyone ever writes a story about me," he said, "I hope it'll be you."

"You mean Grace, not me, right?" Liam said with a chuckle.

Litchfield grew serious. "Speaking of stories, I have some good news to share," he said, sounding oddly sad. "The data terminal works perfectly. We're almost at the finish line—thanks to you two."

Liam grinned despite his remaining reservations. "So what's next?" he asked.

"Another quest?" Grace groaned.

"Yes, actually," Litchfield said quietly.

"It's going to be risky, isn't it?" Liam joked, eyes on Grace.

"Deadly, in fact," Litchfield said. Liam's and Grace's eyes went wide. "But not for you two," Litchfield added.

Both of them wore confused and concerned looks on their faces. Instead of speaking, Litchfield pressed the button to open the secret compartment. Green light filled the room once again. Litchfield beckoned them inside.

Grace proceeded without hesitation. Liam followed cautiously.

The data terminal had been attached to the front of the reactor. A basic visual interface was displayed on the screen. The cursor blinked slowly in the center as if waiting for someone to type something into the keypad at its base.

Litchfield turned to face them. He pointed at the empty space at the device's base. "The missing piece goes here," he said. "But I already have it." He lowered his gaze. "I just need you two to put it in place and type in a password to activate it."

Liam narrowed his eyes at Litchfield. "Why can't you do it?"

Litchfield stared blankly at Liam. "Because I'll be dead."

"What?" Grace cried. "That doesn't make any sense. What's going on, Litchfield?"

Litchfield dropped his hands to his sides. "Please stop calling me that," he said.

The hairs on Liam's neck stood up. All his fears surged toward the surface and gathered in a thick lump in his throat. "Why?" was all he could say.

"It's not my real name. I chose it a while ago in case I met someone. Like you two. I didn't want to scare you off."

Grace tried to hide her growing terror. "You lied to us?"

"Yes," the pale man said, nodding. "About many things. About almost everything—except for one: that this device will work, and it *will* save Asheville."

Liam leaped over to the pale man and grabbed him by the neck. "If you're not Litchfield," he snarled, "then who *are* you?"

"A monster," the pale man said.

CHAPTER
15

Grace took a step back. "What do you mean, you're a monster?"

Litchfield just hung his head.

Liam had no idea what to do. He just stared at Grace, waiting for some sort of direction. Her expression went from shock to hurt to anger and then to wide-eyed despair.

She sat down in a heap next to the so-called Litch-Cell. "You're the reason all this happened to us," Grace said, her voice thick with emotion. "You're the one who designed the faulty reactor." Grace looked up at him with tired eyes. "You're Dr. Kerrigan."

The pale man nodded. Liam released his grip as the room began to spin. "I was off celebrating when the reactor went critical," Kerrigan said. "A flaw in my design. My fault. Countless lives lost. The world changed forever. All because of me."

Grace looked to Liam, expecting him to be seething with rage. But the expression on her friend's face was solemn. Liam placed one hand on a wall and said, "So for all these years you lived like this, trying to make up for your mistake."

"No," Kerrigan said with conviction. "There is no making up for what I did. No fixing it." He placed his hand on the Litch-Cell. "But I can turn things around again. I die tonight."

Grace snapped to attention. "Killing yourself isn't going to solve anything."

"No, I'm not going to kill myself," Kerrigan said. "You are."

Liam stared at him.

Kerrigan glanced at Liam, and then at Grace. "I needed the data terminal to connect the reactor to the Internet. It will interface with the other reactors that are nonfunctioning or disabled across the entire world."

"What?" Grace asked. "Why?"

Kerrigan fixed his eyes on her. "To save the world," he said. "The other reactors will scrub any lingering radiation—and pass on my schematics for modifying the other reactors to function just like this one."

Liam wilted. "I . . . this is . . ." he trailed off. His gaze met Kerrigan's. "Why didn't you tell us this was bigger than Asheville?"

Kerrigan frowned. "I figured it'd be too much," he said. "I didn't want you to get overwhelmed. You two already doubted me."

Kerrigan lifted the Litch-Cell, walked over to where Liam was sitting, and set it down in front of him. "For the sake of the future, Liam, I need you to be a hero. I need you to insert this into the reactor's base. It is the final piece to the puzzle. It will serve as its power source."

Liam looked at the glowing object in front of him, then up at Kerrigan's face. "Your—your soul?" Liam stammered.

Kerrigan nodded grimly in the sickly green light. "So many lost their lives because of my mistake," he said. "It's kind of poetic that

I end up sacrificing mine to help others, don't you think?"

Grace stood. "There's no other way? What happened was terrible, but it was also an accident, right?" Grace asked, her voice rising with each word. "You don't have to do this. You don't have die." A tear ran down her cheek.

"I do," Kerrigan said. "This was the plan from the start. You two coming along was a happy circumstance. I finished the reactor in time to save Asheville—and made two friends. Friends who've reminded me why I spent decades alone, toiling endlessly with scant hope of ever succeeding in my goal."

Liam stood. "Okay," he said. "I'll help you."

Kerrigan nodded. "Thank you." He walked over to Grace and looked her in the eyes. "I'll need your help, too," he said. "You'll have to key in the activation code after Liam activates my device. The final step."

Grace frowned. "So I have to kill you," she said.

Kerrigan frowned. "Probably. But then again, who knows?" He tilted his head. "Maybe part of me will live on in the reactor. Maybe I'll haunt the machine like some ghostly mechanic, like . . ."

Grace smiled weakly. "Like magic."

Kerrigan smiled. "Which just so happens to be the activation code. That's 'magic' with a lowercase *m*."

Grace smiled. She glanced at the book she'd given to the man she'd called Litchfield. It lay unopened on the desk.

"You'll never get to read the book I brought you," she said.

Kerrigan shook his head. "I read it many years ago. But believe me, the sentiment was appreciated."

Kerrigan led them both into the chamber. Liam carried the Litch-Cell into the room while Grace followed forlornly.

Kerrigan fell into a chair in the corner, looking every inch the weary, 150-plus-year-old man he was. Without looking up, he pointed at an outlet on the wall. "The tube connected to the reactor hooks up to that outlet through the terminal. It will connect to the pylons and begin the radiation diffusion and absorption process by providing the pylons with the reactor's power." He pointed at the empty space at the base of the reactor. "That is where you'll place my . . . the Litch-Cell," he said to Liam.

Neither of them said anything. Kerrigan leaned back in his chair and rested his hands on his thighs. "Is everything clear?" he asked.

Grace and Liam nodded.

"I want to thank you both for your help," Kerrigan said. "Liam, you were right to doubt me—I did lie to both of you. You have a keen ability to read others." He paused. "I hope you can forgive me."

Liam glanced at Grace. "Of course," he said without taking his eyes off her. "I understand."

Kerrigan nodded. "That means a lot to me." He looked up at Grace. "Ready?"

Kerrigan didn't meet her gaze, but a solitary tear streamed down his cheek. Grace stood and approached the keypad. Liam nodded at her, and she nodded back.

Liam lifted the Litch-Cell. "Are you ready, Litch—I mean, Kerrigan?" he asked.

Kerrigan nodded. "On second thought, you can call me Litchfield if you like," he said. "After all, you're the ones who'll tell the world this story."

Liam nodded, unsure how to respond. With both hands, he lifted the Litch-Cell and placed it into the reactor. It snapped into place.

Kerrigan stiffened. The sickly-green light in the Litch-Cell began to pulse with increasing intensity and speed . . . and Kerrigan's body began to flake to the ground.

Grace broke into sobs and grabbed Liam's shoulder. "Good-bye," she said to Kerrigan.

Kerrigan nodded. "Good-bye," he whispered, and his lips turned to ash.

The light flared white, blinding Liam and Grace for a long, tense moment. When the light subsided, the two friends opened their eyes.

All that remained of Kerrigan was a pile of ashes on the chair.

EPILOGUE

Liam connected the tube from the reactor to the outlet on the wall. Then he walked back to Grace. Slowly, sadly, Grace typed the word *magic* into the keypad.

Immediately, white fluid flowed out from the reactor, through the tube, and through the outlet, where it would provide power for the pylons outside.

Liam wrapped his arms around Grace, and they stood in silence, waiting for something to happen. But in that compartment, nothing changed. It was just two friends holding each other, standing over a pile of ashes of a man who had ruined and then saved the world.

After what seemed like an eternity of silence, Grace led Liam by the hand out of the chamber, up the stairs, and into the moonlit night.

What they saw made them gasp. The borealis-like lights in the sky had been overcome by a phosphorescent haze. They watched in awe as the white fog wrapped around the green lights, embracing and then absorbing them.

"It's working," Grace said softly. "He's a hero."

Liam wrapped his hands around her from behind and tucked his chin into her neck.

"You're the hero," he said. "If it hadn't been for you, I never would've helped Kerrigan. I might've even hurt him. Asheville would have been doomed. The world would be . . ." He couldn't even wrap his head around it, let alone say it.

Grace turned around to face him. She smiled that smile that made Liam feel full. "And you stood by me," she said. "That makes you a hero, too, doesn't it?"

Before Liam could respond, Grace wrapped her arms around his waist and kissed him.

Afterward, they gazed up at the sky, and then at each other. Grace looked deep into Liam's eyes, and he stared back into hers. For a long moment, neither of them blinked.

Then, there among the ruins of a lost city, beneath the roiling sky, Liam kissed her back.

MELTDOWN TOWN